Ancient Civilizations

THE MESOPOTAMIANS

by Elizabeth Andrews

WELCOME TO DiscoverRoo!

This book is filled with videos, puzzles, games, and more! Scan the QR codes* while you read, or visit the website below to make this book pop.

popbooksonline.com/mesopotamians

abdobooks.com

Published by Pop!, a division of ABDO, PO Box 398166, Minneapolis, Minnesota 55439. Copyright © 2023 by Abdo Consulting Group, Inc. International copyrights reserved in all countries. No part of this book may be reproduced in any form without written permission from the publisher. DiscoverRoo™ is a trademark and logo of Pop!.

Printed in the United States of America, North Mankato, Minnesota.

102022
012023

THIS BOOK CONTAINS RECYCLED MATERIALS

Cover Photo: Universal History Archive/Contributor, Shutterstock Images

Interior Photos: Shutterstock Images, Getty Images, North Wind Picture Archives/Alamy Stock Photo, Dorling Kindersley/Getty Images, Historia/Shutterstock, Classic Image/Alamy Stock Photo, Gianni Dagli Orti/Shutterstock

Editor: Emily Dreher

Series Designer: Laura Graphenteen

Library of Congress Control Number: 2022941119

Publisher's Cataloging-in-Publication Data

Names: Andrews, Elizabeth, author.
Title: The Mesopotamians / by Elizabeth Andrews
Description: Minneapolis, Minnesota : Pop!, 2023 | Series: Ancient civilizations | Includes online resources and index.
Identifiers: ISBN 9781098243296 (lib. bdg.) | ISBN 9781098243999 (ebook)
Subjects: LCSH: Middle East--History--Juvenile literature. | Ancient civilization--Juvenile literature. | Indigenous peoples--Social life and customs--Juvenile literature. | Cultural anthropology--Juvenile literature.
Classification: DDC 972.01--dc23

*Scanning QR codes requires a web-enabled smart device with a QR code reader app and a camera.

TABLE OF CONTENTS

CHAPTER 1
Sumer: The First Civilization 4

CHAPTER 2
Assyria and Babylon............. 10

CHAPTER 3
Life and Religion 16

CHAPTER 4
Advancements and
Innovations 22

Making Connections............. 30
Glossary 31
Index........................... 32
Online Resources 32

CHAPTER 1

SUMER: THE FIRST CIVILIZATION

Mesopotamia was home to the world's first civilization. The historical region was located between the Tigris and Euphrates Rivers at the meeting point of three continents. It was the perfect location for people to gather and begin human civilization. Through its long history, many civilizations rose and fell.

WATCH A VIDEO HERE!

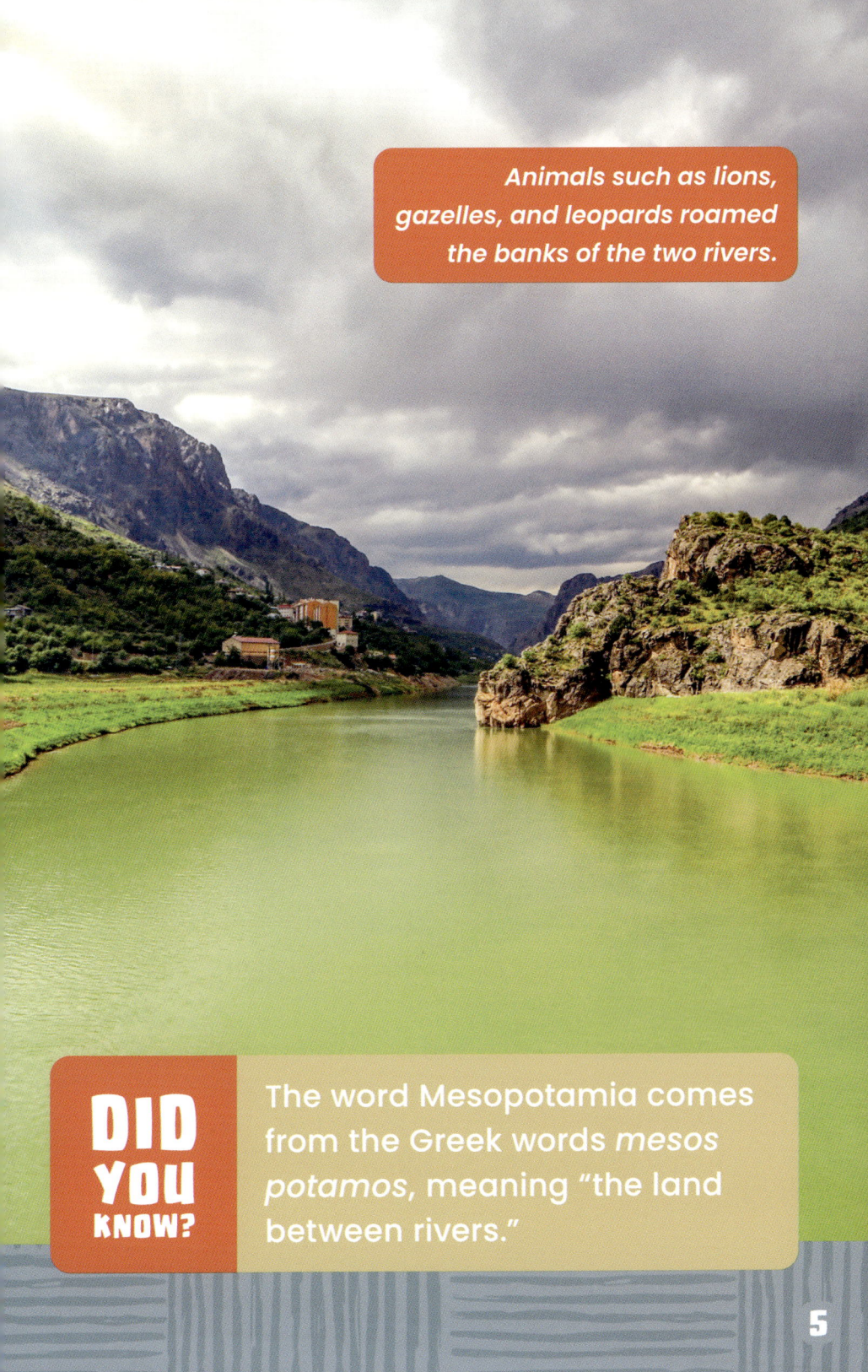

Animals such as lions, gazelles, and leopards roamed the banks of the two rivers.

DID YOU KNOW? The word Mesopotamia comes from the Greek words *mesos potamos*, meaning "the land between rivers."

In 5400 BCE, the oldest city in the world, Eridu, started in southern Mesopotamia. Ancient people believed the gods created the city. The people of Eridu were the first to perfect **agriculture**.

Eridu had good access to fresh water and **fertile** soil.

After another 1,400 years, the city of Ur was formed. Ur became the **cultural** center of Mesopotamia. More cities popped up and eventually joined together to become the Sumerian civilization. Cities were ruled by local **dynasties**.

EPIC OF GILGAMESH

The *Epic of Gilgamesh* is the oldest example of written fiction in history. It is a poem written by ancient Mesopotamians and took 1,100 years to complete. Many different people wrote it. The poem is about King Gilgamesh who was part god. The king turns bad but **redeems** himself and overcomes death.

In the early 2300s BCE, Sumer was taken over by the Akkadian empire. The two civilizations blended into one. But Akkad did not stay the strongest ruling culture in Mesopotamia for long. It crumbled at the hands of violent tribes in 2004 BCE.

Cities in the Sumerian and Akkadian civilizations were walled and usually had a ziggurat in the middle. They each

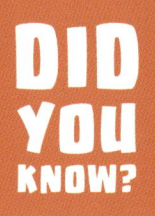

DID YOU KNOW? The time between Sumer and Babylon is the same time between Babylon and today.

worshipped their own gods. People were identified in a **caste** system of rulers, slaves, and laborers. Laborers were potters, tailors, stonemasons, brewers, farmers, or other tradesmen. They had their own written and spoken languages.

Ziggurats were Mesopotamian pyramids with steps on the outside. They often had temples at the top.

CHAPTER 2
ASSYRIA AND BABYLON

While southern Mesopotamian empires were growing and changing, people also spread north. They settled new cities. In 2500 BCE, the cities of Nineveh and Ashur were the first of the Assyrian empire.

LEARN MORE HERE!

Meanwhile, Babylon, a city that began as a part of Sumer in 2290 BCE, became the new **cultural** center of Mesopotamia.

This gate was the main entrance to the great city of Babylon.

In 1792 BCE, a king named Hammurabi joined together cities under his rule and spread the Babylonian empire. Babylon was the biggest city in the world. It was famous for its large

Babylon was full of courtyards and gardens behind its brick walls.

 **DID YOU KNOW?** The Code of Hammurabi is a famous written collection of laws dating back to 1771 BCE.

ziggurats, successful **agriculture**, and gardens. Arts, sciences, math, music, and literature thrived in the city.

When Hammurabi died, the following kings were not strong enough to keep the empire. For 800 years the Assyrians from northern Mesopotamia existed alongside the Babylonians. There were wars, and different groups fought for control of Babylonian land. But Assyria took control after Hammurabi died.

Assyrians were powerful. Their civilization was famous for how strong their warriors were. In 911 BCE, they began **conquering** lands around them. Assyria united most of the area now known as the Middle East. Assyria ruled this region for 300 years.

When the Assyrian capital of Nineveh fell in 612 BCE, Babylon once again rose to greatness. Its military conquered places all over, including places now called Syria and Palestine. King Nebuchadnezzar II rebuilt the capital city with stronger

The Hanging Gardens of Babylon are considered one of the Seven Wonders of the Ancient World.

walls, new ziggurats, and the famous Hanging Gardens of Babylon. In 539 BCE the Persian empire attacked Babylon and ended the final civilization of ancient Mesopotamia.

CHAPTER 3
LIFE AND RELIGION

As different civilizations came and went during the 5,000 years of Mesopotamian history, daily life continually changed. Basic life was similar for commoners. They would wake up, pray, and work. There were some upper-**caste** citizens

EXPLORE LINKS HERE!

who owned businesses and employed others. They would have free time to do as they pleased. Scribes and tutors were also part of the upper caste.

Ziggurats were often the center of life in Mesopotamian civilizations.

Gods in Mesopotamia had human traits and were similar sizes to people. They would rule over heavenly bodies, like the moon and sun, and other natural

All wind was thought to come from Enlil's mouth.

things, such as wind, water, and animals. The gods and goddesses had human needs for food and homes, but they could never die. The gods allowed all good and bad things to happen in the civilizations.

Important gods and goddesses changed during Mesopotamia's long history. Each civilization that came to power brought their chosen god with them. Enlil was the most important god when the Sumerians ruled. He was the Lord of Air. When Babylon was most powerful, Marduk was the chief god.

Gods and goddesses were worshipped in ziggurats dedicated to them. **Priests** would perform **sacrifices**, blessings, and predictions of the future. People in the priesthood held a lot of power in Mesopotamian civilizations. They were the most educated in any city. Many priests were women who became rulers of cities. The only people more powerful than them were the kings.

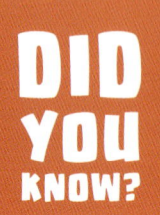 **DID YOU KNOW?** Priests and priestesses watched the skies for changes with the sun, moon, and stars.

Beautiful collections of jewelry were unburied in Ur.

CHAPTER 4

ADVANCEMENTS AND INNOVATIONS

Sumerians were the first people to use irrigation. They dug channels and changed the landscape to move water to their crops. It was the beginning of **agriculture**. This allowed people to settle in permanent communities.

COMPLETE AN ACTIVITY HERE!

People only had hand tools and their own strength to harvest crops when agriculture began.

The communities needed animals to help with the farming. Oxen plowed fields. Goats provided food and milk. Sheep provided wool. All other creatures could be used as food or clothing. These things were needed for a civilization to be born.

Villages existed before the first Sumerian city of Eridu. But Eridu was

As time went on, communities in Mesopotamia grew into large and beautiful cities.

the first community where housing, agriculture, and religion combined in one place. This made it the world's first civilization. It had walls to keep its people safe, and it had public streets and markets. With this kind of setup, people lived in enough comfort to develop even more technologies.

Once civilization began, it continued to grow into new cities and powers. The Sumerians made another important invention, writing. They made the first known writing system in the world. Writing tracked trade, ownerships, and government records. Mesopotamians wrote on soft clay tablets with a reed.

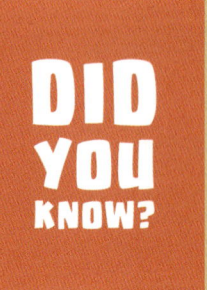

DID YOU KNOW? Scribes wrote with simple characters that represented goods, animals, places, numbers, and business transactions.

A story called the **Epic of Gilgamesh** *is the earliest example of long fiction.*

The tablet would be left to harden.

Eventually poems, books, and even music were written!

Weapons and tools were first made of stone then copper, bronze, and iron. People were able to become better farmers and build stronger armies with these tools. Mesopotamians also invented things such as the potter's wheel, clay bricks, looms for making clothes, and measurements of time. They gave us the second, minute, hour, and day!

The land of Mesopotamia is called "the cradle of civilization." It was the setting for many of the world's firsts.

Humans would not know the world as it is today without the civilizations of Mesopotamia.

Mesopotamians used spears, axes, daggers, and bows and arrows.

MAKING CONNECTIONS

TEXT-TO-SELF

Do you think writing or farming was more important of an invention? Explain your answer.

TEXT-TO-TEXT

Have you read any other books about ancient civilizations? If so, what did they have in common with Mesopotamia?

TEXT-TO-WORLD

What made Mesopotamia a perfect place for civilization to begin? Do the same qualities exist in that location today?

GLOSSARY

agriculture — growing and harvesting crops and raising animals, or livestock.

caste — social positions one is born into. Opportunities one has depends on their caste.

conquer — to gain land by force.

cultural — of or relating to the customs, arts, and tools of a nation or a people at a certain time.

dynasty — a series of rulers from the same family.

fertile — producing plentiful crops.

priest — a person who oversees ceremonies, prayers, and offerings to the gods.

redeem — to change for the better.

sacrifice — the act of offering something to a god or goddess to please them.

INDEX

agriculture, 6, 7, 13, 22, 24–25
Akkad, 8–9
art, 13
Assyria, 10, 13–14

Babylon, 6, 9, 11–15, 19

Eridu, 6–7, 24–25
Euphrates River, 4, 6

Hammurabi, 12–13
Hanging Gardens of Babylon, 15

religion, 6, 9, 18–20, 25
Sumer, 7–9, 11, 19, 22, 24, 26

Tigris River, 4, 6
time, 28

war, 13–15, 28
writing, 7, 9, 13, 26–27

DiscoverRoo! ONLINE RESOURCES

This book is filled with videos, puzzles, games, and more! Scan the QR codes* while you read, or visit the website below to make this book pop.

popbooksonline.com/mesopotamians

*Scanning QR codes requires a web-enabled smart device with a QR code reader app and a camera.